*For Grace,*
*who helped me to think like a truck*
—E. B.


*For Patricia Doktor Jackson*
—B. E. J.

Henry Holt and Company, *Publishers since 1866*
Henry Holt® is a registered trademark of
Macmillan Publishing Group, LLC
175 Fifth Avenue, New York, NY 10010
mackids.com

Text copyright © 2019 by Elise Broach
Illustrations copyright © 2019 by Barry E. Jackson

Library of Congress Cataloging-in-Publication Data
Names: Broach, Elise, author. | Jackson, Barry (Barry E.), illustrator.
Title: Bedtime for Little Bulldozer / Elise Broach ;
illustrated by Barry Jackson.
Description: New York : Henry Holt and Company, 2019 |
"Christy Ottaviano Books." | Summary: A young bulldozer
struggles to fall asleep.

Identifiers: LCCN 2018020977 | ISBN 9781250109286 (hardcover)
Subjects: | CYAC: Bulldozers—Fiction. | Bedtime—Fiction.
Classification: LCC PZ7.B78083 Be 2019 | DDC [E]—dc23
LC record available at https://lccn.loc.gov/2018020977

Our books may be purchased in bulk for promotional, educational,
or business use. Please contact your local bookseller or the Macmillan
Corporate and Premium Sales Department at (800) 221-7945 ext. 5442
or by e-mail at MacmillanSpecialMarkets@macmillan.com.

First edition, 2019 / Designed by Patrick Collins
The artist used pencil and Adobe Photoshop to create the
illustrations for this book.
Printed in China by RR Donnelley Asia Printing Solutions Ltd.,
Dongguan City, Guangdong Province

10 9 8 7 6 5 4 3 2 1

# Bedtime for Little Bulldozer

ELISE BROACH    illustrated by BARRY E. JACKSON

Christy Ottaviano Books

Henry Holt and Company ✦ New York

Little Bulldozer was finally ready for bed.

He'd taken a bath, with help from his mother.

He'd brushed his teeth, with help
from his father.
    And together they had checked
all of his fluid levels.

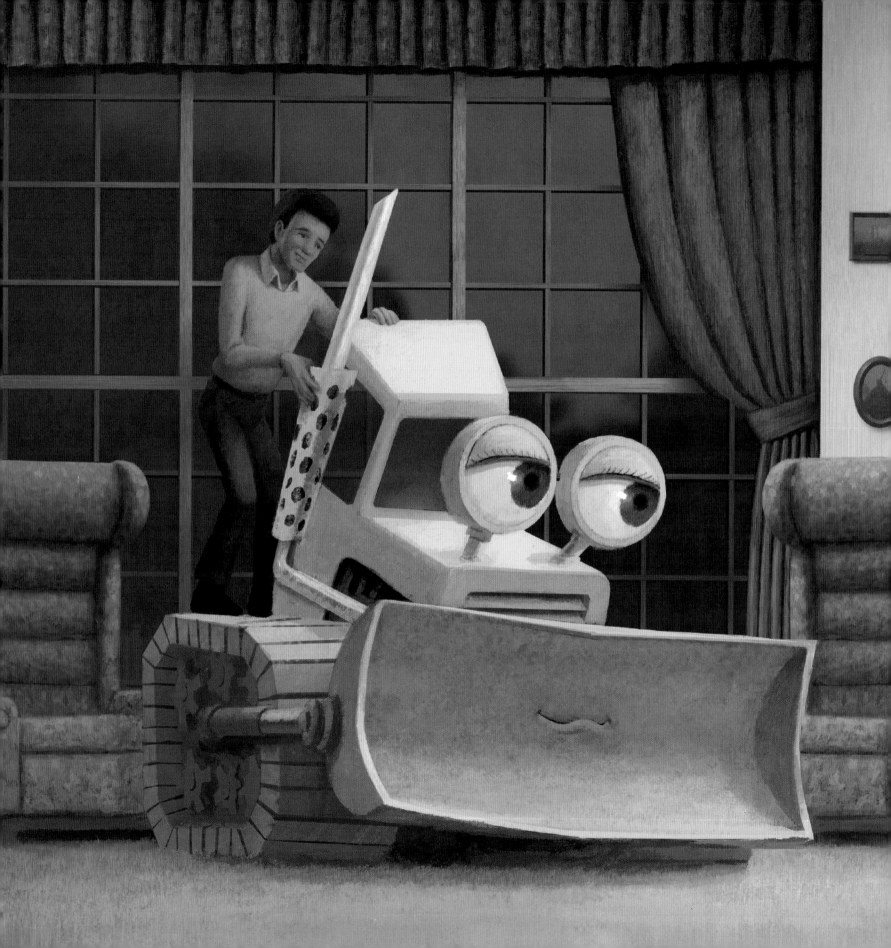

Now his mother and father kissed him and hugged him and said good night. "Time for bed!" they told him.

He tried his best to go quietly up the stairs.

Vroom, Vroom!

Little Bulldozer was all ready for bed.
There was just one problem.
He wasn't sleepy AT ALL.

He was too hot, so he used his blade to push off his covers.

Then he thought he heard something under the bed, so he decided to have a look.

Creak!

BUMP!

Phew. There was nothing underneath except his stuffed animals.

Little Bulldozer's mother and father
came running into the room.

"Little B!" they cried. "What happened?
You should be asleep."

They helped Little Bulldozer fix his bed.
Then they kissed him and hugged him
and said good night.

Little Bulldozer lay in the dark,
quiet room.
   He still wasn't sleepy.
   In fact, he was a little chilly.
   So he shoveled his stuffed
animals on top of the bed,
making it comfy and cozy.

Good! Now he was warm again.
But he still wasn't the least bit sleepy.

He turned on his headlights and found a
book to read. Luckily, it was his favorite book.

It was such a good book that Little Bulldozer got very excited and honked his horn a few times.

His mother and father rushed into the room. "Little B! That's too loud! Why aren't you asleep yet?"

He was thirsty, so they
gave him some oil. His cab
was cold, so they put on
his nightcap. Then they
kissed him and hugged
him and said good night.

Little Bulldozer lay
in the dark, quiet room,
still
   not
      sleepy.

He could hear his mother and father in the living room. He decided to tiptoe downstairs to see what they were doing.

They weren't as happy to see him
as he had hoped.

"Little B, IT IS TIME FOR BED!"
said his mother.

"No more stalling!" said his father.

Little Bulldozer lay in the dark, quiet room.
He tried to go to sleep. He really did.
But something still wasn't quite right.

He was lonely.

Suddenly, he knew
exactly what to do.

He scooped up his
blanket and his stuffed
animals and rumbled
down the hall, until
he came to the room
where his sisters were
sleeping.

He cleared a place for himself
on the floor . . .

And there, in the safe, crowded dark,
to the hum of his own engine . . .

Little Bulldozer fell asleep.

ZZZ-ZZZ
ZZZ-ZZZ
ZZZ-ZZZ